Animals That Change

Written by Jo Windsor

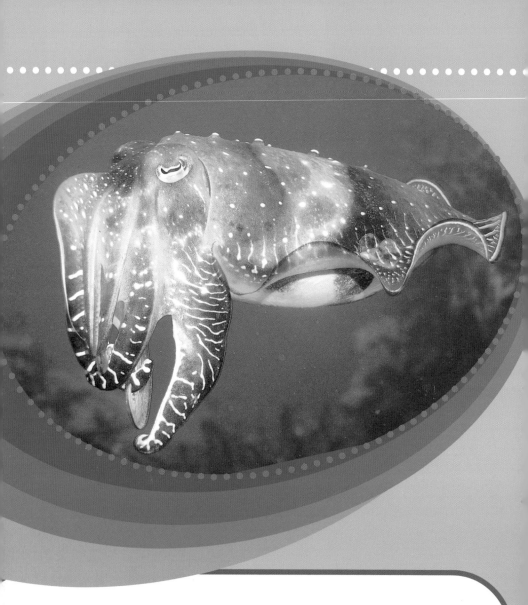

Look at this animal.

cuttlefish

Look at this animal now.

Look at this animal.

lizard

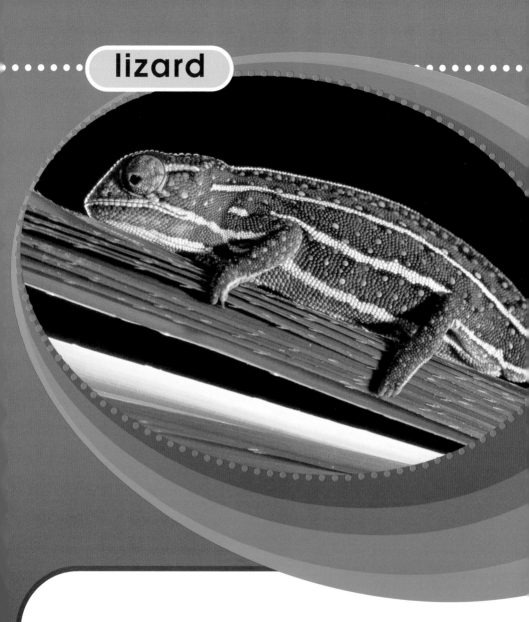

Look at this animal now.

Look at this animal.

octopus

Look at this animal now.

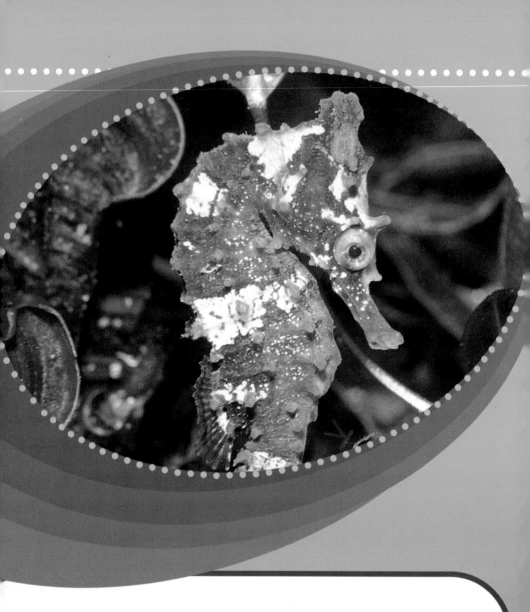

Look at this animal.

sea horse

Look at this animal now.

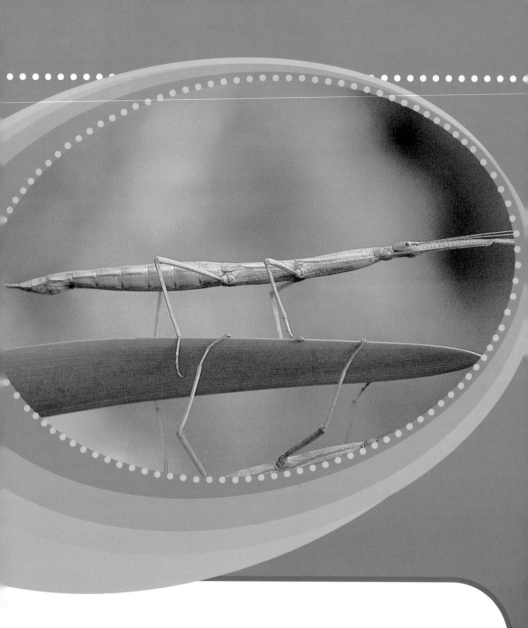

Look at this animal.

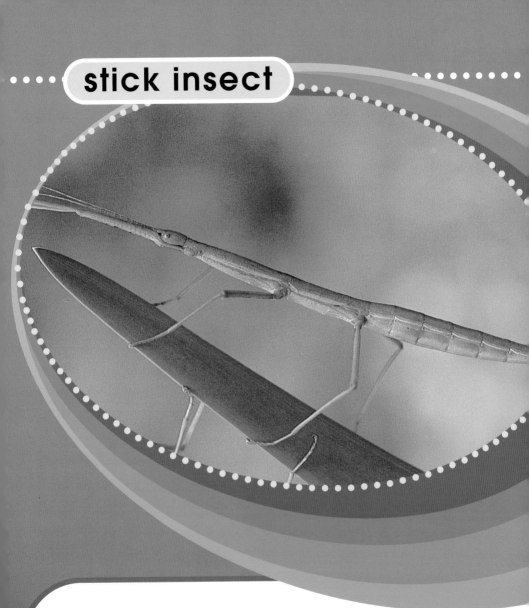

stick insect

Look at this animal now.

Look at this animal.

frog

Look at this animal now.

Index

cuttlefish 2-3

frog 12-13

lizard 4-5

octopus 6-7

sea horse 8-9

stick insect . . 10-11

■■■■ Guide Notes

Title: Animals Can Change
Stage: Emergent – Magenta

Genre: Nonfiction (Expository)
Approach: Guided Reading
Processes: Thinking Critically, Exploring Language, Processing Information
Written and Visual Focus: Photographs (static images), Index, Labels
Word Count: 54

FORMING THE FOUNDATION

Tell the children that this book is about animals that can change colors.
Talk to them about what is on the front cover. Read the title and the author.
Focus the children's attention on the index and talk about the animals that they will see in the book.
"Walk" through the book, focusing on the photographs and talk about the changes that the children see. For example, on pages 2-3. Look at this animal. Look at this animal now.

Read the text together.

THINKING CRITICALLY

(sample questions)

After the reading
- Why do you think the animals have changed color?
- What animals do you know that can't change color?

EXPLORING LANGUAGE

(ideas for selection)

Terminology
Title, cover, author, photographs

Vocabulary
Interest words: animal, now
High-frequency words: look, at, this